Robot Spike's
First Halloween Party

written and illustrated by
RYAN DEBOY

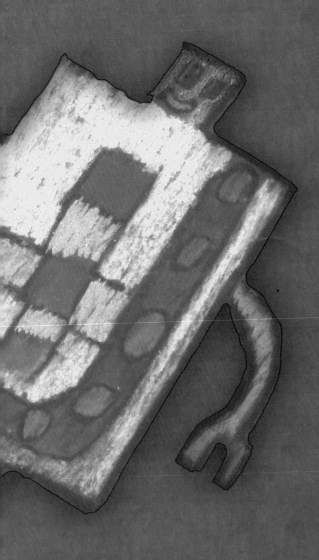

First published by Dog Ear Publishing
4010 W. 86th Street, Ste H
Indianapolis, IN 46268
www.dogearpublishing.net

ISBN: 978-160844-992-7

This book is printed on acid-free paper.

Printed in the United States of America

I would like to dedicate this book to
the teachers I have had
at West View Elementary School,
especially Mrs. Cantrell and
Mrs. Shadoin.

~

I would also like to greatly thank
Dog Ear Publishing
for their help and support.

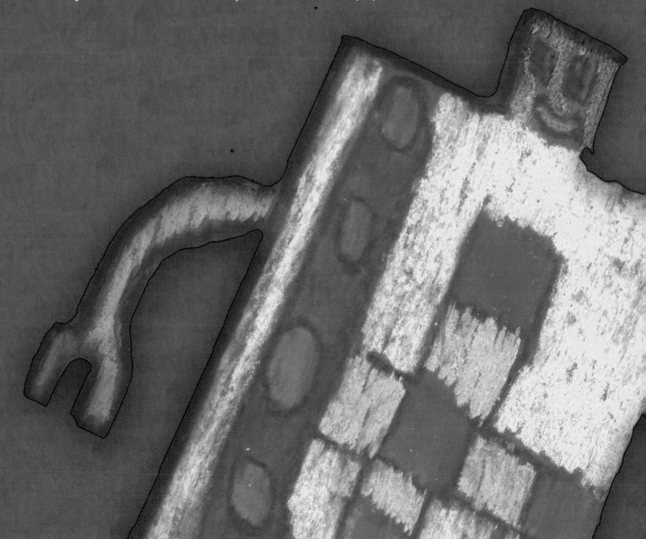

There was only one day before

Halloween!

Spike was very excited for
Halloween because he was having
his first Halloween party.

Spike is a

gold and ice blue robot

that likes drinking uranium.

He is ten feet tall and
likes eating oil cookies.

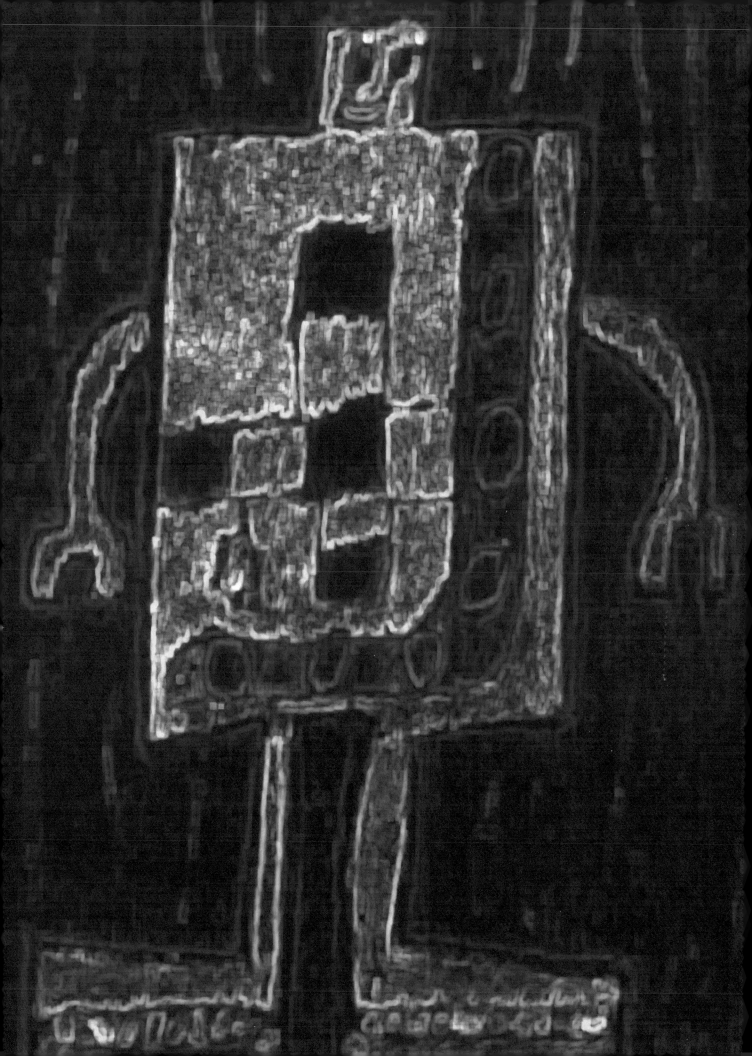

Spike lives in

Ooze Town.

Ooze Town is a town
that doesn't have day or night.
All day is just a

total eclipse.

Brown and purplish red ooze
drips out of the sidewalks.

Almost all the adults looked

Spike's house looks like a crashed
rocket ship.

It was part metal and part wood.
A great place for a robot.

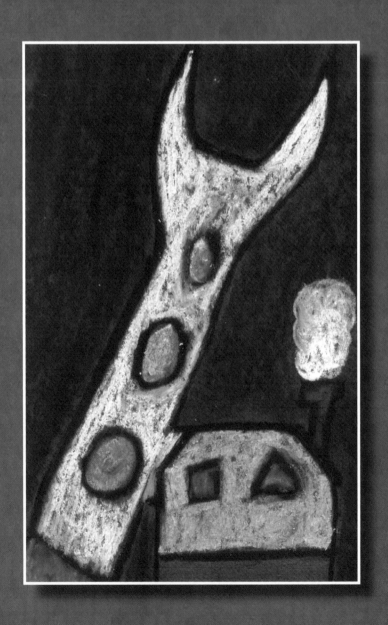

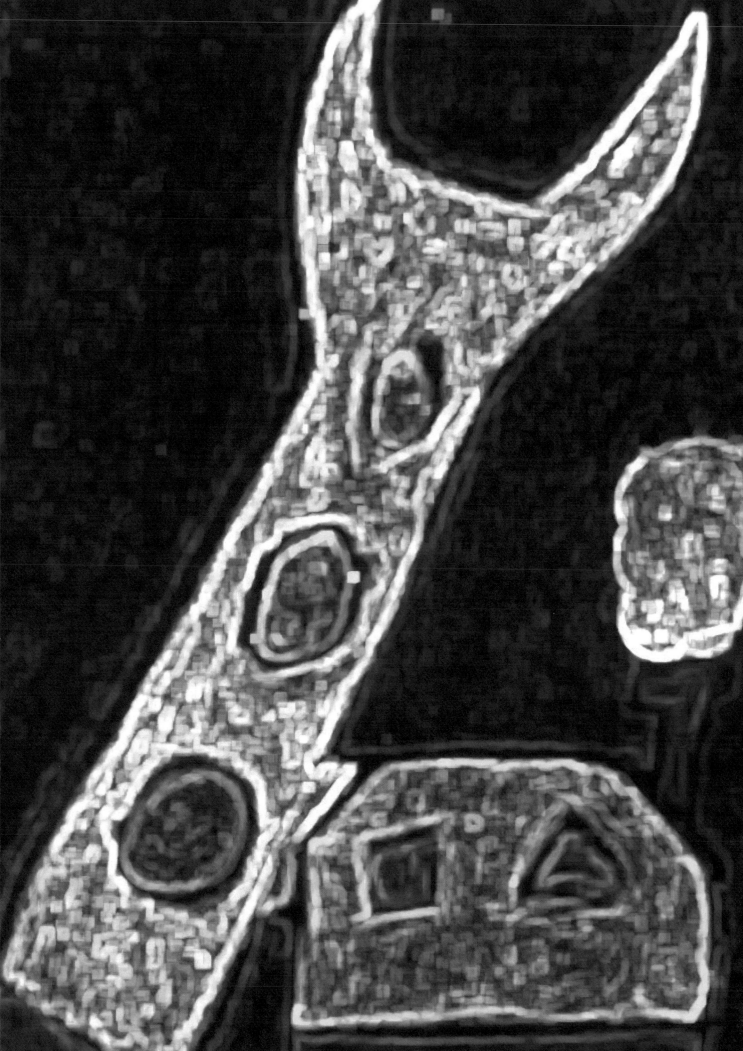

His house is all ready for the

Halloween party.

He has live

hanging from the ceiling.

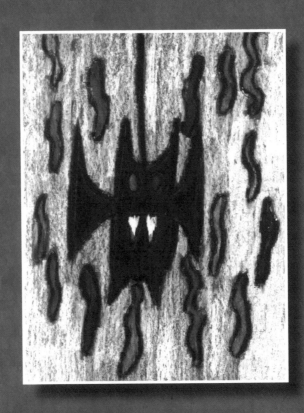

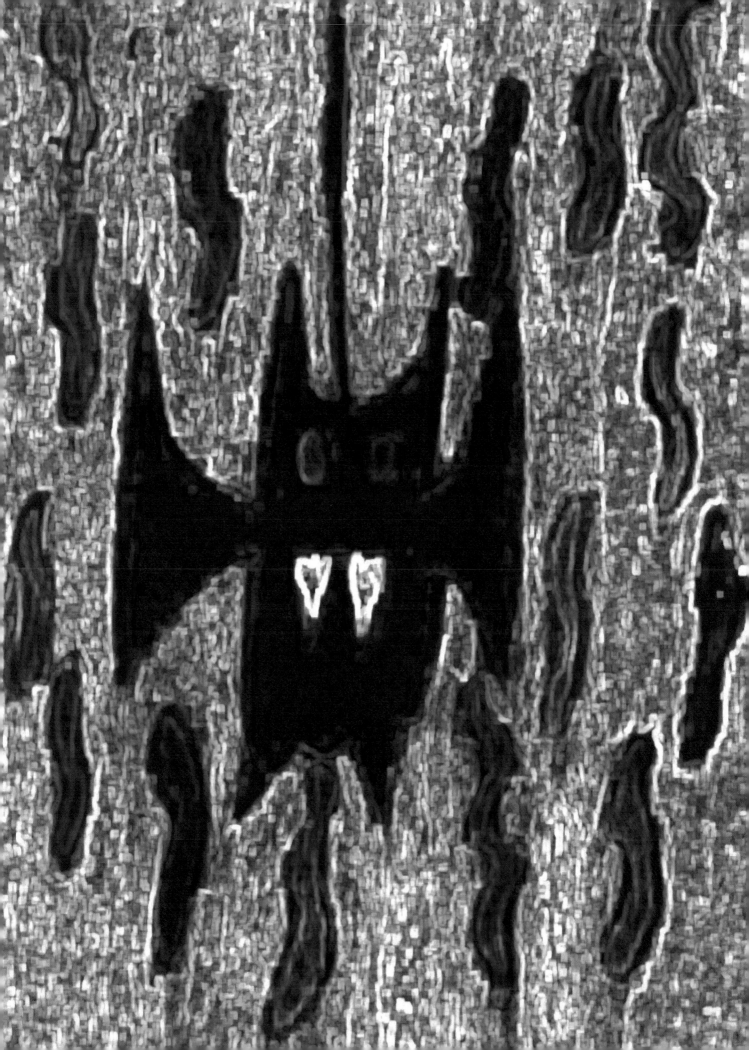

He has

100 jack-o-lanterns

inside and outside his house.
He has paid

30 ghosts

to swoop around his house
the night of the party.

Last night he hung up

WORM LIGHTS

around his dance floor
in the basement.

Dead Bones

and his band will entertain
his guests.

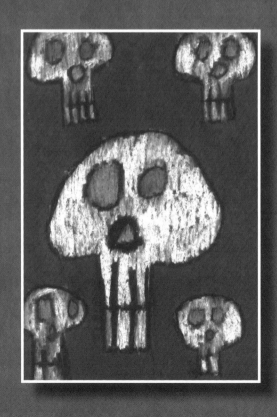

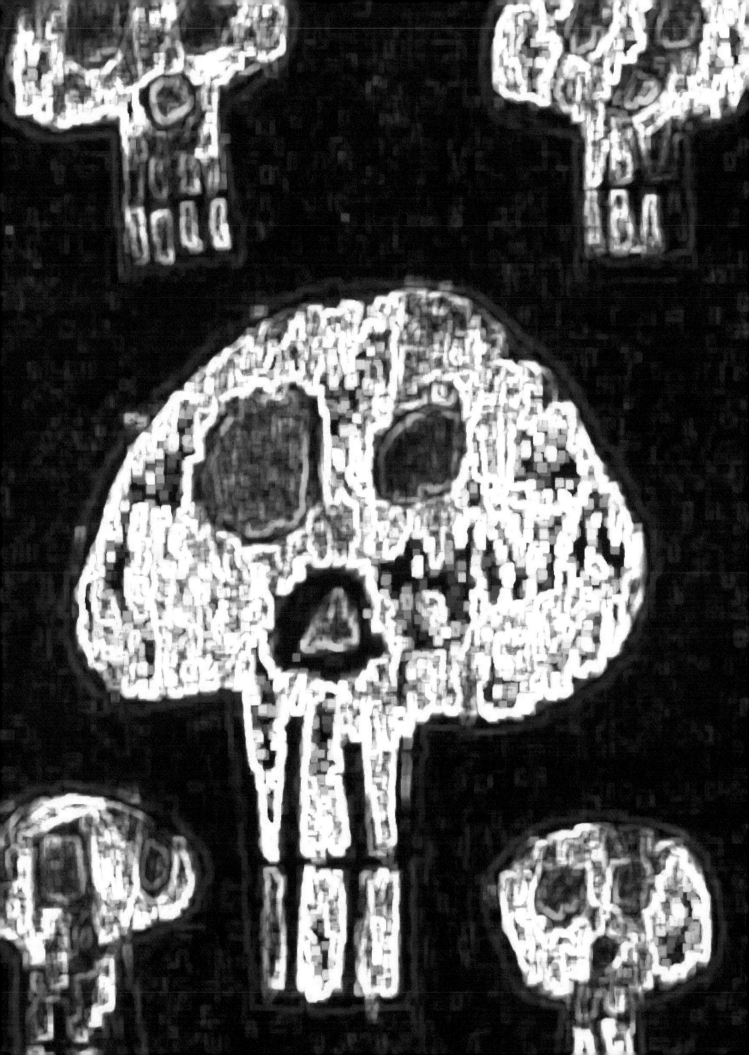

Spike ordered four pepperoni and

cheesy eyeballs

pizza to come at midnight.

That is when all his guests
would arrive for the party.

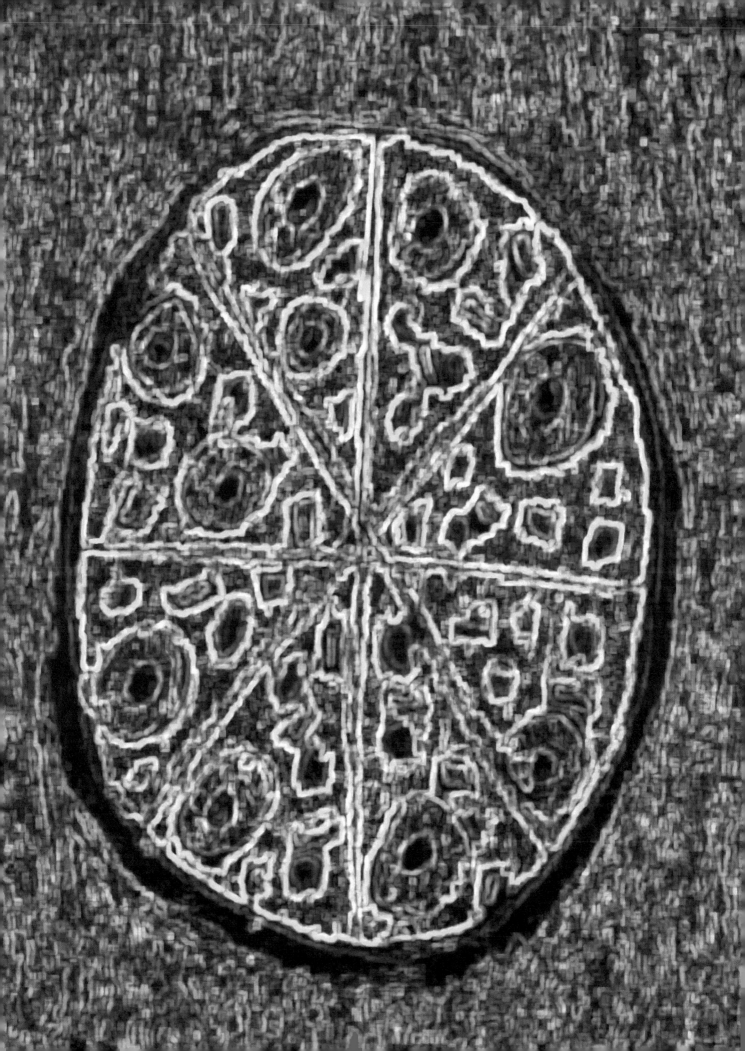

At midnight, his best friends

reptoid and oni

were the first guests to arrive.

Reptoid wore a big black cape to cover
his green bony back and a short
spiky black wig to create his

dracula costume.

Big white fangs finished
his scary look.

Oni had made
funny brown ears
to cover his horns
so he could be a
werewolf.

Spike scared them
with his costume
by dressing as

Bigfoot!

Finally,
everyone arrived at the party
and they all had a

screaming

good time.
All the guests danced
and moaned to the

horrifying music

played by

Dead Bones

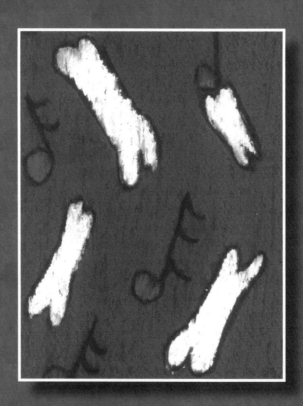

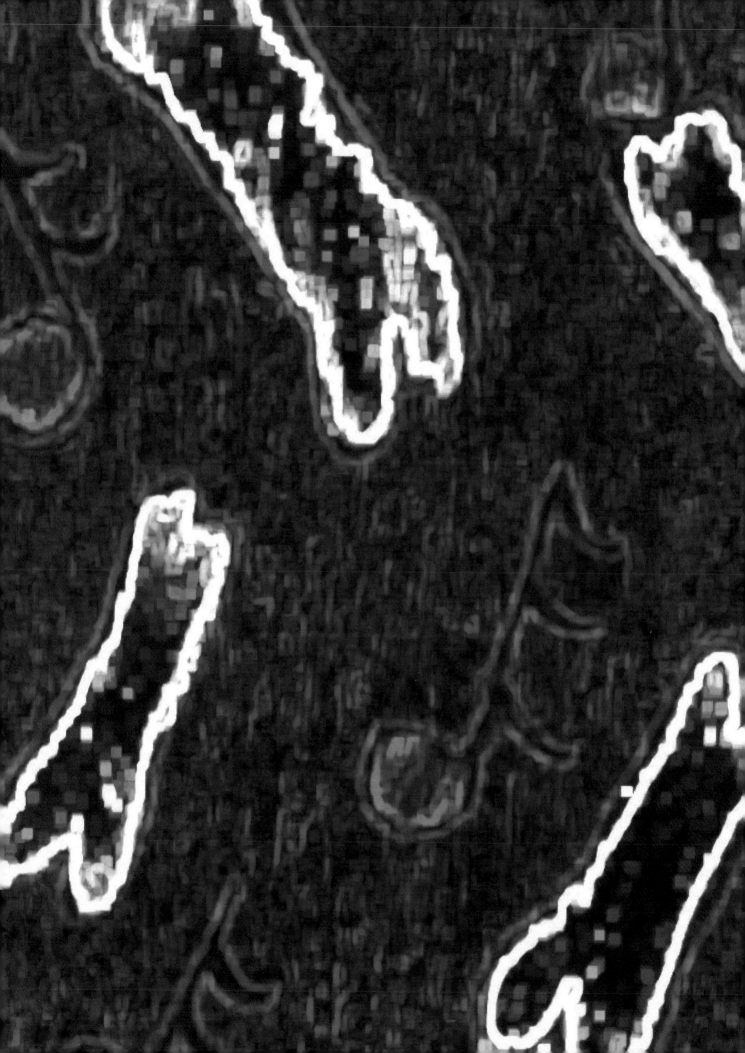

They played

gross games

and had a

howling and
shrieking

contest.

Guess who won?

EVERYONE!

CPSIA information can be obtained
at www.ICGtesting.com
Printed in the USA
237248LV00002B